This book belongs to:

..............................................

# MR WALKER

### and the Dessert Delight

*For Vanessa, with so much gratitude.*
*You gave us our forever home* – JB

*For Daisy Walker* – SA

PUFFIN BOOKS

UK | USA | Canada | Ireland | Australia
India | New Zealand | South Africa | China

Penguin Books is part of the Penguin Random House group of companies
whose addresses can be found at global.penguinrandomhouse.com

Penguin
Random House
Australia

First published by Penguin Random House Australia Pty Ltd, 2019

Text copyright © Penguin Random House Australia 2019
Illustrations copyright © Sara Acton 2019

The moral rights of the author and the illustrator have been asserted.

Cover design by Kirby Armstrong © Penguin Random House Australia
Typesetting by Midland Typesetters, Australia
Printed and bound in China

A catalogue record for this
book is available from the
National Library of Australia

ISBN 978 0 14379 308 3

penguin.com.au

# MR WALKER

## and the Dessert Delight

## JESS BLACK
### Illustrated by Sara Acton

PUFFIN BOOKS

# CHAPTER ONE

Mr Walker felt his stomach catapult to the ceiling before plummeting down to his paws. Luckily, as the lift drew to a standstill, his tummy was right back where it should be. The doors opened with a *whoosh* and Mr Walker was greeted with his reflection in the opposite wall of polished chrome and mirrors.

*You look like a friendly chap*, he thought to himself.

The man beside Mr Walker in the reflection was none other than Henry Reeves, the manager of the hotel where they both lived.

'No time for daydreaming, Mr Walker,' Henry said brightly. 'We have a big day ahead of us.'

As far as Mr Walker was concerned, every day at Park Hyatt was a big one. There were always new people to meet, strange smells to sniff and the potential for more than one walk if he played his cards right.

Mr Walker followed Henry as he strode across the marble floors. Henry's shoes made a bold *clip-clop* sound. Once upon a time, Mr Walker felt clumsy on such a slippery surface, but he now walked confidently on the shiny marble. He was pleased to see Omid, the Head Concierge, deep in conversation with Monica, who also worked on the front desk. His day was already looking up as Omid and Monica were two of his favourite people.

'Good morning, Henry. Morning, Mr Walker,' Monica said, smiling from ear to ear. 'We have some fantastic news to share with you.'

Mr Walker listened with interest. He wondered if it might involve food or walks, or both.

'Grethe Schmidt has confirmed she is arriving tomorrow morning,' Monica said, beaming.

'Brilliant news,' Henry agreed. 'She's very busy promoting her new cookbook, so we're lucky to get her.'

'And you're certain that Remy will be okay with the idea?' Omid asked, looking unsure.

At the mention of Chef Remy and food, Mr Walker's ears pricked up. Food was his favourite topic and eating was his favourite pastime, with walks and sleep coming a close second and third.

Henry gave a firm nod. 'Absolutely. Remy is a professional. I'm sure he'll relish the opportunity to share his kitchen with someone of Grethe's talent.'

Omid raised one eyebrow but remained quiet.

*I wonder what that's about,* thought Mr Walker. He cocked his head and looked quizzically at Omid and Henry.

'We were just discussing some of the details

for the hotel's birthday party,' Omid said to Mr Walker.

*Party?* Mr Walker liked parties. He was particularly fond of parties that involved lots of food.

'Our hotel is turning twenty years old, so we thought we should celebrate,' Henry explained. 'We're always hosting other people's parties, but this time everyone who loves staying here will be celebrating the hotel.'

Twenty years did sound like a long time to Mr Walker. After all, he was only two years old in human years and fourteen years old in dog years. Twenty sounded very grown-up. He had never had a birthday party of his own and it sounded terribly exciting.

Monica produced a white card filled with fancy, silver lettering. It read:

*You are invited to join us for the 20th anniversary of Park Hyatt Melbourne. As a valued guest of the hotel, we would like to offer you the opportunity to attend a three-course dinner in celebration of this milestone.*

Henry rubbed his hands together, looking pleased. 'It's perfect, Monica. Just perfect.'

Mr Walker agreed. It sounded most impressive and he couldn't wait for the big day. After all, everyone loves a party and Mr Walker was no exception.

# CHAPTER TWO

Mr Walker followed Henry as he wound his way through the numerous corridors that led to the hotel kitchen. Mr Walker particularly enjoyed this route as it was always rich with scents. He could detect the smell of eggs scrambling in a hint of truffle oil, and fluffy pancakes drizzled in maple syrup.

*Mmm.* Mr Walker loved pancakes!

'Could you wait here for a minute, Mr Walker?' Henry said as they approached the swinging kitchen door. 'I need to have a word with Remy.'

Mr Walker was well schooled in where he could and could not go in the hotel. He was welcome in the back offices, the laundry press and even on the tennis court, but he was never to step foot into the kitchen or restaurant.

He settled onto the plush carpet with a sigh and listened to the familiar sounds of a busy kitchen. There was the usual chatter among the staff, the sizzling of pans and the clanging of ladles against metal pots. There was also the distant ring of a bell announcing a new order.

*Boy, does it smell good today*, Mr Walker thought, his tummy rumbling in agreement. He knew firsthand that Remy was a most excellent chef who took great pride in his work. Mr Walker also knew Remy could be a little temperamental and had what people called a temper. It seemed that being eccentric came with the territory.

Suddenly, a loud *crash* sounded from inside the kitchen.

'No, no, no, no, NO!' Remy yelled in a thick French accent.

There was a loud *smash* and an even louder *bang!*

Mr Walker winced and shook his head. Due to his exceptional hearing, any loud noise sounded catastrophic to him.

'Grethe Schmidt?' Remy thundered.

*Clang!*

'German pastry chef?' Remy roared.

*Bang!*

'She is no chef!' Remy howled. 'She is a mere celebrity!'

*Kebang!*

A second or two passed before Mr Walker peeked out from behind his front paws. There was no more banging and crashing and yelling. Mr Walker stood up and trotted towards the kitchen door. He nudged it open with his nose and was relieved to see that Henry was still in one piece.

With flushed cheeks, Henry retreated to the hallway and took a moment to collect himself. 'I think that went rather well,' he said, 'don't you?'

Mr Walker had a sinking feeling in his stomach. Grethe Schmidt was due to arrive the very next day and Remy's reaction was less than encouraging.

10

# CHAPTER THREE

It had indeed been a busy day and Mr Walker was now happily curled up in his bed with his beloved wombat toy. Luckily, after Remy's outburst, the kitchen had returned to its normal service. Henry had worked hard to placate the chef, assuring him that Grethe's presence would help him with his workload for such an important event.

Mr Walker and his family had begun watching Grethe's show since learning she would be coming to the hotel. The show was very popular, and through it Mr Walker learned plenty of things about Grethe. Not only was she a talented pastry chef, but she was also a wonderful singer. Mr Walker liked her colourful outfits too. In his experience, chefs wore a plain white uniform with a stiff white hat. Not Grethe Schmidt! Her uniforms were bright and cheerful, which matched her bubbly personality.

'It's almost time, girls!' Mrs Reeves called, settling onto the couch.

'Coming, Mum!' Amanda's voice grew louder as she dashed into the room and bounced into the spot next to Mrs Reeves.

Sophie followed close behind and took her place on the floor next to Mr Walker, giving his soft ears a tickle as she did so. His tail thumped softly on the plush carpet with appreciation. Mr Walker loved tickles!

'Hello, my *liebchens*,' Grethe called from

the television. 'Thank you for joining me today in my darling kitchen!'

Sophie giggled. She liked the way the woman spoke and how she used the word 'darling' for everything.

Mr Walker felt the same way. He enjoyed listening to Grethe's sparkly voice and watching her eyebrows dance as she spoke.

'Today I am going to make something called ze Paris–Brest.' Grethe held up a finished example. The pastry was round and filled with what looked to be cream. Mr Walker licked his lips. 'See how it is shaped like a bicycle wheel?'

'It does look like a bicycle wheel,' Amanda said, leaning forward in her seat.

Mrs Reeves nodded. 'I do believe it does!'

'This darling dessert was created in 1910 to celebrate the long-distance bicycle race from Paris to Brest and back again,' Grethe explained. 'And I can tell you, my friends,

I would much rather make pastries *for* the race than ride *in* the race!' The German chef threw her head back and laughed heartily.

'I wonder how long it takes to ride a bike from Paris to Brest,' Sophie said.

It was as if Grethe heard her through the television. The chef went on to describe how the race was famously gruelling, spanning over a thousand kilometres and involving many hills. Mr Walker imagined that the riders would be very hungry by the time they finished. Tucking into a delicious pastry sounded like the perfect meal indeed.

'Can we have a go at making a Paris–Brest, Mum?' Sophie asked.

Mrs Reeves bit her lip. 'Oh . . . I'm not sure. I suspect Grethe Schmidt makes it appear much easier than it actually is.'

Amanda's eyes lit up. 'I know! Maybe Grethe could make it with us.'

Mr Walker thought that was a terrific idea. His tail began to *swish*, *swish*, *swish* back and forth on the carpet in excitement.

Sophie circled her arms around her mother's waist and gave her a fierce hug. 'Can we? Please?'

Mrs Reeves returned her daughter's hug. 'I'll speak to your father, but I can't promise anything. With the anniversary party just a week away, Grethe will be very busy.'

'YES!' both girls chorused in unison.

'And here it is,' Grethe's voice tinkled. She held up her final product, a round dessert made from choux pastry and filled with praline mousseline cream. It was decorated with flaked almonds and powdered sugar.

Mr Walker's mouth drooled at the thought of biting into the soft pastry. He wasn't the only one.

'I don't know about you, girls,' Mrs Reeves said, getting to her feet, 'but after watching that, I think we need to tuck into something sweet.'

Mr Walker's ears pricked up. *Yes, please!*

'Ice-cream?' Sophie suggested.

'Ice-cream!' Mrs Reeves agreed.

Mr Walker closed his eyes and drifted off to sleep to the sound of spoons clinking against bowls as the chocolate and vanilla ice-cream rapidly vanished.

# CHAPTER FOUR

Mr Walker's whiskers danced. He waggled his nose, squeezed his eyes shut and sure enough ... *Archoo!*

'Bless you,' Thomas murmured without looking up from the crossword.

*Thank you.* Mr Walker settled back onto his bed next to the porter's station at the front entrance to the hotel.

Thomas was concentrating very hard. He loved doing the newspaper crossword every day and Mr Walker loved helping him as he too liked words and the meanings behind them. Mr Walker had learned lots of new words this way. For instance, he now knew the meaning of the words 'discombobulate', 'flabbergasted' and 'hunky-dory'. They were long words and knowing their meaning made him feel cleverer.

Mr Walker sniffed the air. His sneezes were often the result of strong perfume or too much pollen in the air. A wave of flowery sweetness blew his way.

*Archoo!*

'Four down and three across,' Thomas said, chewing the end of his pencil. 'Thirteen letters. Iconic French dessert.'

Mr Walker loved desserts. He gave the question some serious consideration, but thirteen letters seemed an awful lot. Chef Remy would certainly know the answer.

He rose as Henry's car pulled into the bottom of the long driveway. The fact that Henry had personally driven to the airport to meet Grethe revealed just how important a guest she was.

'They're here!' Thomas gasped. He quickly folded the newspaper and tucked it into the side pocket of his uniform. He picked up the telephone and dialled the concierge desk. 'Henry is pulling up now,' he informed Omid.

Thomas replaced the receiver and ran his hands through his hair. He tucked in his shirt and straightened his waistcoat.

Mr Walker stood up and gave his body a great big shake. *That's better*, he thought, and trotted over to greet their latest guest.

Thomas opened the back door with a flourish and Mr Walker was met with the very colourful sight of Grethe Schmidt.

The celebrity chef was even more vibrant in person than on television. She wore a buttercup-yellow dress and lilac ballet flats. Her blonde hair was cropped and her lips were painted a bold red. Mr Walker thought she looked very glamorous.

'Welcome to Park Hyatt, Ms Schmidt,' Thomas said with a ready smile.

Mr Walker never tired of hearing Thomas say these four magical words. He always made it sound as if he was saying them for the very first time.

Grethe stepped out of the car and gasped when she saw Mr Walker. Before he knew what was happening, she had cupped his face in her palms and planted a kiss on his furry snout. Mr Walker inhaled her scent – a combination of cinnamon and freshly baked bread. Delicious. He wanted to fall into her arms and sleep for a week.

Henry chuckled at the look of surprise on the Labrador Ambassador's face. 'This is Mr Walker,' he said. 'He is arguably our most charming employee.'

'How lucky you are, Henry, to live with such a handsome hound!' Grethe exclaimed. Her deep-blue eyes twinkled like stars.

Mr Walker sat up tall. He couldn't help but fall completely in love with Grethe, who clearly had excellent taste in people and dogs. He hadn't even eaten one of her pastries yet. There was so much to look forward to! So much indeed.

# CHAPTER FIVE

Word had spread like wildfire around the hotel that the rather delightful Grethe Schmidt had arrived and was resting in her room on the twenty-second floor. Henry had reserved their best suite for her and Elvis had even triple-checked the room to make sure everything was spotless and shipshape.

All staff were on high alert, waiting with anticipation for the German pastry chef to make her appearance. Of course, what they were most interested to see was how Remy would conduct himself when the two chefs met for the first time.

Rumours had been circling. Monica swore she had spied Remy watching Grethe's show on repeat and shouting angrily at the television. Omid reported that Remy had bought a brand-new uniform for the occasion. One of the kitchenhands said Remy had been sharpening his kitchen knives with an intensity in his eyes that had never before been seen.

It was almost lunchtime when Mr Walker exited a functions meeting and was nearly bowled over by the exquisite smells wafting from the kitchen. He had no choice but to follow it to its source. He wasn't alone. A small crowd had gathered around the kitchen doors.

Elvis held a finger to his lips, then peered through the small round window in one of

the doors. Beside him, Meraj stood on her tiptoes to steal a peek. Omid looked slightly sheepish at being caught eavesdropping. He offered Mr Walker a chair to stand on so that he could see what all the fuss was about.

The first thing that Mr Walker noticed was the silence. The banging and clanging that had become customary over the past week had ceased. Mr Walker could see Henry standing in between Grethe and Remy as they all studied a sheet of paper.

'Henry had an idea that Remy and Grethe could get to know each other by preparing the menu together,' Elvis explained.

Mr Walker gulped. It sounded like a good idea in theory, but goodness knows how it would actually turn out. He studied Grethe, who was chatting and laughing. He then turned his gaze to Remy, who looked calm and composed. Remy nodded thoughtfully and added a suggestion, which the others immediately seemed to like. In fact, Remy and Grethe's body language indicated that they were getting on very well. Mr Walker felt hugely relieved. Now they could all pour their energies into the hotel's anniversary party.

Henry placed the menu on the kitchen counter and left the chefs to carry on.

'Quick!' Monica gasped as Henry headed for the exit. 'Find something to do!'

Mr Walker jumped off the chair and onto the carpet. Omid scooped up the chair and returned it to its original position. Elvis pulled a feather duster from his back pocket and began fussing over a wall light. Monica whipped out her phone and pretended to be having a conversation.

Mr Walker wasn't sure what he should do to look busy, so he turned in circles.

'Just look natural,' Elvis whispered. 'Act casual.'

So Mr Walker did what he always did when he felt his most relaxed. He curled up in a ball in the middle of the hallway and closed his eyes.

The door swung open and Henry appeared. He took in the scene before him. Omid was rearranging a chair, Elvis was dusting a lamp and Monica was engrossed in a call while, at their feet, Mr Walker appeared to be fast asleep.

'Show's over, folks! I think you'll find that our two chefs are getting on like a house on fire,' Henry said, looking chuffed. He strode off, chuckling to himself.

There was a slight pause before Elvis whispered, 'He's gone.'

Mr Walker opened his eyes.

Monica let out a deep breath and put away her phone.

Omid pushed his glasses up the bridge of his nose. 'Henry's right,' he muttered, shaking his head. 'There is much to do. Let's get to work, people!'

Mr Walker watched the three of them disappear around the corner, then approached the kitchen door with caution. He nudged the frame so it opened just a fraction but not enough for him to be seen. He poked his snout inside and sniffed.

Yes, the kitchen was full of the usual delicious aromas, but there was a whiff of disharmony in the air. Grethe's cinnamon scent clashed with Remy's more pungent spicy aroma like two bulls in a pen.

*Oh no*, thought Mr Walker. He may have made many mistakes in the past, but his sense of smell had never let him down. While Henry might not want to think there was a problem, Mr Walker's nose was telling a very different story.

# CHAPTER SIX

Later that morning, Mr Walker and Thomas were busy sorting the deliveries for the party. Mr Walker stood guard over the contents while Thomas loaded crates and boxes onto a trolley to take into the hotel. There were boxes upon boxes of decorations, fresh linen and gourmet ingredients for the grand dinner.

'I have to say, Mr Walker,' Thomas puffed, returning from his fifth trip carting supplies from the footpath to the foyer, 'I'm glad that twentieth anniversaries only come around every twenty years.' His cheeks were flushed from the effort.

Mr Walker flashed him an encouraging smile. All of the staff were going above and beyond to make sure the event was a success.

Thomas took a sip of water and glanced down at his newspaper. 'By the way, I finally figured out that word we were stuck on.'

Mr Walker's ears pricked up. He remembered it was a thirteen-letter word for an iconic French dessert. He had thought of éclair and crème caramel, but neither of those words were long enough.

FRESH LOBSTER

'It's a croquembouche,' Thomas declared triumphantly. 'I asked Remy and he got it straight away. Apparently, it's his favourite dessert. It's made up of a tower of profiteroles that are piled into the shape of a cone and bound together by threads of spun sugar. Doesn't that sound divine?'

*Divine indeed*, thought Mr Walker. It sounded positively scrumptious.

'Right, back to work. You're in charge, Mr Walker.' Thomas grunted as he tilted the trolley onto its two rear wheels and pushed off. 'I'll be back in a jiffy.'

Mr Walker was intrigued by the pile of assorted containers, from cardboard

boxes to straw baskets. He sniffed them, trying to guess their contents. He could smell nougat and marzipan, various ground nuts as well as chat potatoes, black olives and parsnips. His tummy grumbled at the thought of all the dishes they would make.

Catching a whiff of rosewater and freshly whipped cream, Mr Walker looked up to see Grethe Schmidt approaching. She was wearing a gingham skirt and a hot-pink blouse complete with sky-blue kitten heels.

'*Guten Tag*, Mr Walker!' She waved and hurried over to give his ears a hearty ruffle. 'I will take this teensy-weensy box inside myself,' Grethe said, plucking a tiny pink carton from the pile. 'No need to mention this to Thomas or Remy,' she added with a wink.

*What is Ms Schmidt up to?* Mr Walker wondered as the woman tottered off. He hoped he wouldn't get in trouble for letting her take the box. She was a very special guest, after all, and it was a very small box. Surely there would be no harm done.

As soon as Grethe had disappeared, Remy appeared on the scene. The French chef was as unlike Ms Schmidt as it was possible to be. While she was all colour, he was always dressed in his chef whites. Where she was blonde with pale skin, he had short black hair and olive skin. Remy's eyebrows didn't dance when he talked; his were solid and steady like Remy himself. But Mr Walker had always liked and respected the man. He kept his kitchen clean and efficiently run and his staff respected him.

'*Bonjour*, Monsieur Walker,' the Frenchman said with a nod. He paused to scan the load of supplies. 'You are well, yes?'

*Very well, thank you.*
Mr Walker wagged his tail.
It was rare to see Remy outside
his kitchen.

'Aha!' Remy's eyes lit up as
he spotted a bright purple
container. He plucked it
from the pile and held his
finger to his lips. 'Just between us, *s'il vous plaît*, Monsieur Walker.'

With growing unease, Mr Walker wondered what was going on. Why were Remy and Grethe sneaking supplies and why, oh why, was he stuck in the middle?

That night Mr Walker heard the front door open and close quietly. It was late; Mrs Reeves and the girls had already been asleep for hours. Henry sank into the couch with a sigh. In the glow of a lamp, Mr Walker could just make out the man's face. He looked awfully tired.

Mr Walker trotted over and placed his head on Henry's lap. Henry reached down and patted Mr Walker on the head. 'I see now there is a reason for the saying "too many cooks spoil the broth",' Henry said.

It was Mr Walker's turn to sigh. He had been afraid this might happen.

'What a day, Mr Walker.' Henry sat back and yawned. 'I have two of the best chefs in the world and they're playing childish games. Today, in some ridiculous attempt to keep their dishes secret, they hid ingredients from one another. By doing so, they sabotaged our guests' dinners. I had three separate tables complain about their meals!'

*Oh dear*, thought Mr Walker. *That is not good. Not good at all.* He wanted very much

to make Henry feel better. He lifted a paw
and placed it on Henry's knee.

'Can you imagine Skillet Tarragon
Chicken without the tarragon, or potato-
and-leek soup without the leek?' Henry ran
his hands through his hair in exasperation.
'It cannot go on . . .'

Mr Walker let out a sympathetic whine.

'Well, tomorrow's another day,' Henry said, rising to his feet. He yawned again and stretched. 'Thank you for the talk, Mr Walker. Goodnight.'

*Goodnight, Henry.* Mr Walker returned to bed and curled around his toy wombat, while Henry turned off the lamp, once again bathing the room in moonlight.

# CHAPTER SEVEN

Remy might not have been a fan of Grethe Schmidt, but there were at least two little girls in Park Hyatt who thought the world of the German pastry chef. Her presence in the hotel had ignited a love of baking in Sophie and Amanda Reeves.

Their mother held up the book and inspected the recipe with a frown. 'I don't even know where to begin with something like profiteroles,' Mrs Reeves admitted.

She reread the instructions for creating the delicate layers of choux pastry.

'It looks easy, Mum,' Sophie said, pointing at the page. 'We just have to make the pastry and then pipe in the filling.'

'Mmm, easy-peasy,' Mrs Reeves said doubtfully.

Mr Walker peered up at the picture. The pastries looked to be balls of just the right size for him to chase and then swallow. He decided he liked profiteroles very much.

There was the telltale rattling of a key in the lock before the front door opened to reveal Henry and Grethe Schmidt. Grethe stepped inside and clapped her hands. 'Oh, this is too gorgeous!' she exclaimed.

The girls squealed with delight and raced across the room to give the woman a hug.

'Are you going to bake with us?' Amanda asked breathlessly, while Sophie jiggled up and down beside her.

Grethe grinned. 'It would be my pleasure, little ones. What did you have in mind?'

Mrs Reeves held out the cookbook. 'Apparently, profiteroles are easy.'

Grethe raised an eyebrow. 'I wouldn't say easy,' she replied, laughing, 'but I would say delicious! Show me the kitchen and we will get to work.'

Mr Walker, Mrs Reeves and the girls spent a few fun-filled hours learning how to make profiteroles with Grethe. The recipe was complicated, and the balls needed two days of preparation. They were

cleaning up the mess they had made when there was a sharp rap on the front door. Henry, who had been working on his laptop at the dining table, got up to answer it. Mr Walker padded out into the sitting room and was surprised to see a furious Chef Remy standing in the doorway with his arms crossed.

'Oh, hello, Remy,' Henry said. 'Is everything all right?'

'No, Henry, everything is far from all right,' Remy replied, his left eye twitching with anger. He strode into the room and proceeded to pace up and down the length of it. He threw his arms into the air and gestured wildly. 'Ms Schmidt is impossible! I refuse to work with that woman!'

Henry glanced back towards the kitchen and cleared his throat. 'Perhaps we should speak in the hall,' he whispered. 'The kids are in the next room.'

But Remy didn't seem to hear him. 'She . . . she . . . she has completely rearranged my kitchen,' he thundered, jabbing his chest with his thumb. 'MY kitchen!'

'Ah, I see,' Henry said quietly.

Remy stopped pacing and fixed Henry with a hard look. 'A cook's kitchen is his castle. My knives go here, my spoons go here and my pots go there. I have a system, Henry. When I am cooking for one hundred people at a time, I cannot be fumbling around, trying to find the right equipment.'

A whine escaped from Mr Walker's lips. He hoped Ms Schmidt couldn't hear what was being said.

'She moved *everything*,' Remy continued. 'Now the pots are down here, and the sauces are arranged alphabetically – and the pantry! Do not get me started on the pantry!'

Henry sighed wearily. 'All right, Remy, I'll speak to Grethe. I'll sort it out, I promise.'

There was a pause before Remy added, 'She is not a real chef, Henry. She is a *celebrity*. It is all hot air and painted nails.'

Mr Walker heard a loud gasp and turned to find Grethe, Mrs Reeves and the girls standing in the kitchen doorway.

'I see,' Grethe said icily. 'At least now I know *exactly* how you feel, Mr Charron.'

Remy's cheeks burned red. He gave a curt nod and left the room.

Mrs Reeves put her hand on Grethe's shoulder. 'Let's have a cup of tea,' she said, and gently steered the woman back into the kitchen.

Henry held his head in his hands and groaned.

Mr Walker had a bad feeling in the pit of his stomach. He padded over to Henry and rested his head against Henry's leg. They needed to find a way to make Remy and Grethe to work together, but how?

## CHAPTER EIGHT

If Remy and Grethe had been behaving like children before, the events of the previous day did nothing to ease the tension. Grethe's solution was simply to pretend the Frenchman did not exist and, of course, Remy retaliated in turn. Instead they both chose to communicate through Charlie, the beleaguered assistant chef.

Mr Walker happened to be walking past the restaurant as the chefs were prepping for lunch. He wouldn't normally break the rules, but decided to poke his head in to see how the situation was faring.

'Could you ask Chef Charron to pass ze parmesan cheese?' Grethe said to Charlie, as she stirred a pot of cream on the stove for her parmesan mousse.

Charlie looked nervously from Grethe to Remy. Remy rolled his eyes and handed him a block of parmesan cheese. Charlie passed the cheese to Grethe.

'Thank you, Charlie,' she replied brightly.

Remy was busy putting the finishing touches to his famous beef bourguignon. 'Charlie, can you ask Ms Schmidt to pass me ze red wine?'

With a harrumph, Grethe picked up the bottle, strode over to the pot and poured half of its contents into the dish.

*Uh-oh.* Mr Walker could hardly bear to watch. He didn't know what the recipe

required, but he was sure this could only spell bad news.

'What are you doing?' Remy shrieked, tearing at his hair.

'I can tell it needs more flavour,' Grethe said. 'But then what would I know? I am all hot air!' She threw him a look that was pure poison and disappeared into the storeroom.

Charlie stood frozen to the spot, his mouth hanging open.

Remy stared into the pot with a frown and half-heartedly stirred the dish. 'It is ruined,' he said through gritted teeth.

With a heavy heart, Mr Walker watched as Remy poured the dish into the bin and started again from scratch.

Mr Walker had never seen the hotel this busy before. Couriers ran in and out, dropping off parcels in all shapes and sizes. The foyer was filled with the buzz of guests anticipating something very special, and staff raced about, doing their best to make it happen. There were people everywhere. The anniversary dinner was now one night away, and not only was the hotel fully booked, but deliveries for the event were flooding in.

'Coming through!' Elvis called as he wheeled a trolley of fresh linen.

Mr Walker leaped out of the way, almost colliding with Meraj, who had

two enormous vases filled with flowers in her embrace.

'Oops – careful there,' she warned with a smile.

*That was close*, thought Mr Walker.

One look at Henry's frazzled expression and Omid's frown told Mr Walker that the day's events had not brought harmony to Park Hyatt's kitchen. They were huddled together behind the concierge desk, talking in urgent tones. Luckily, Mr Walker had such excellent hearing that, despite all the noise in the foyer, he could still make out what they were saying.

'We have one more night to sort this out,' Henry said, looking very tense. 'This is getting down to the wire.'

'Yes,' Omid replied, 'the hotel is full to the brim and guests for the party will begin arriving tomorrow afternoon.'

Henry shrugged. 'I've tried everything, but they are both adamant that they are to work separately.'

Mr Walker's tail drooped. He felt sad for Henry that the hotel's anniversary was being overshadowed by the rivalry between Remy and Grethe. Mr Walker decided to take the matter into his own paws. After all, the job of a Labrador Ambassador was to help restore peace in times of crisis. He couldn't make anything worse, could he?

# CHAPTER NINE

Being the only dog who lived in the hotel, Mr Walker often noticed things his human companions did not. He could detect when the laundry changed the brand of fabric softener it used, and he could tell from scent alone what the fresh flower arrangements in the lobby would be the minute he set one paw out of the lift.

It wasn't only by smell that Mr Walker made his observations. He knew the inner workings of the hotel like the back of his paw. For instance, he knew when room inspections were taking place on the nineteenth floor, or when the valets in the car park changed shifts.

As he thought back over the last few days, Mr Walker remembered that he had seen Grethe sitting in one of his favourite places in the hotel on more than one occasion. Funnily enough, it was the very same spot Remy often went to enjoy some peace and quiet after a busy day. Suddenly, Mr Walker had an idea.

Although Henry always accompanied Mr Walker on his first walk of the day, staff and guests took a trot with the Labrador Ambassador in the mid-morning and afternoon. On this particular day, it just so happened to be Remy's turn.

Mr Walker made a point of walking slower than usual as they strolled the city streets. He needed to make this walk last as long as possible. Luckily, Remy was so preoccupied that he didn't notice Mr Walker taking a different route to their usual one.

When he was sure it was time, he led Remy up the hotel driveway, through the foyer and into the garden courtyard. Before Remy knew what was happening, he was sitting opposite a startled Grethe, who was about to take her first sip of tea.

Remy shot out of his seat and gave Mr Walker's lead a gentle tug. But the Labrador Ambassador kept his bottom firmly planted on the ground and refused to move.

'I think he wants you to stay,' Grethe said, a smile tickling her red lips. 'How about you share this pot of tea with me, Remy? I've even baked scones to go with it.'

Grethe poured tea into a cup and placed it in front of Remy. She then sliced a warm scone in half and slathered it with freshly whipped cream and a hearty dollop of rose-petal jam. She passed the plate across the table to Remy.

*Go on*, Mr Walker thought. All hope hung on what Remy would do next.

There was a rather long, rather awkward silence before Remy accepted the plate and slowly sank back into his chair.

*Mmmm.* Mr Walker thought it smelled utterly delicious. He wished he was sitting in that chair instead of Remy.

'Mr Walker has a point,' Grethe said. 'Perhaps this has gone on long enough.'

Remy cleared his throat and took a sip of tea. He liked it so much he drained his cup.

'Tea has to be brewed for exactly the right amount of time at exactly the right temperature. You can taste the difference, can you not?' Grethe said, pouring more into Remy's cup.

Remy took a bite of the scone and his eyes widened.

'This is my own recipe for rose-petal jam,' Grethe told him. 'Do you like it?'

Mr Walker hoped a crumb or two would find their way onto the floor.

Remy seemed to be lost for words. 'It is ... excellent,' he said, and meant it.

Grethe nodded, looking pleased. 'My grandmama's recipe. Look, Remy, we do not need to be the best of friends – or even like each other's cooking – but we need to be able to work together. For the sake of the hotel.'

Remy had by now stuffed the rest of the scone into his mouth. 'For the hotel,' he agreed. 'Now, do you have any more of those scones?'

Mr Waker noticed a large crumb fall from Remy's mouth and dived for it. It was very tasty indeed.

# CHAPTER TEN

All too soon, the big night arrived. A string quartet was entertaining guests in the main foyer while waiters wove through the crowd with trays of champagne and scrumptious hors d'oeuvres. As the dress code was black tie, the staff had donned their formal uniforms for the occasion. Henry was in a tuxedo, as was Omid. Monica was wearing a floor-length gown and even Mr Walker had swapped his everyday uniform for a

bow tie. Judging from his reflection in the mirrored lift, Mr Walker thought he looked rather dashing.

Henry stood off to the side, flanked by Monica, Omid and Charlie. Mr Walker stationed himself beside Henry.

'We have exactly fifteen minutes until the guests take their seats, and twenty-five minutes until the entree is served. How are things back of house?' Henry asked in a low voice. He smiled and waved at guests walking by.

'The smoked duck breast and apple salad is good to go,' Monica replied. 'The alternative entree of bresaola, sautéed mushrooms, pine nuts and gorgonzola dressing needs another ten minutes.'

Henry checked his watch. 'What about the mains, Omid?'

Omid read from a printed menu. 'Crispy monkfish with capers needs another thirty minutes, but the shrimp stew and the bouillabaisse are ready.'

Henry nodded. 'Which brings us to the dessert. How is Grethe faring, Charlie?'

The assistant chef gulped and looked a little as if he were choking. Mr Walker surmised he was probably a shy lad and not used to being out of the kitchen.

'Charlie?' Omid prodded him in the ribs.

'Ms Schmidt is, uh, making her, uh, signature German pastry called the Baumkuchen,' the lad squeaked.

'Yes, yes,' Omid said impatiently.

But Charlie was not to be rushed. 'The name translates to "tree cake". It's made by ladling layer upon layer of batter. Each layer has to be grilled before the next layer is poured over it.'

Mr Walker could feel his mouth watering.

'And where exactly is Grethe in this process?' Henry asked nervously.

Charlie smiled. 'Oh! The cake is made and it's nearly four-feet tall! Ms Schmidt has coated the final cake in a chocolate glaze.'

Mr Walker had watched the tree cake grow and grow over the past day. It was indeed a sight to behold.

Henry, Monica and Omid breathed a collective sigh of relief.

'I'm not one to count my cakes before they bake, but it sounds like we're on track,' Henry said, wiping his spectacles with his handkerchief. 'Now, I should get back to welcoming our guests. Please do your best to encourage everyone to take their seats by quarter to seven.'

The others nodded their understanding and dispersed into the crowd. Charlie almost ran back to the kitchen.

Henry turned to Mr Walker. 'We all have an important role to play tonight, you included. As you know, we wouldn't normally allow you into the restaurant, but for tonight I'm happy to make an exception. We couldn't have an anniversary celebration without our Labrador Ambassador, so I've arranged for you to accompany Grethe as she brings out her dessert. How does that sound?'

*Tiptop!* Mr Walker could not have been happier to be given such an honour and, what's more, he'd be in prime position for cleaning up any crumbs that made their way to the floor!

The contented murmur of laughter and conversation said it all. Not to mention the scrape of knives and forks on plates as guests polished off Remy's first two courses with gusto.

Mr Walker was also taking this rare opportunity to mop up the kitchen floor with his tongue. He sniffed out every morsel of porcini, every shaving of truffle and even managed to hunt down a stray slice of pepperoni.

Meanwhile, Remy and Grethe waited with bated breath. They watched the kitchen doors until, finally, a line of waiters laden with cutlery and plates streamed through.

'Another satisfied customer, Chef Remy!' one of the waiters said, holding up a perfectly empty plate.

Remy's eyes lit up and he clapped his hands. 'Fantastic!' he cried, and turned to Grethe. 'Ms Schmidt, it is time. What can I do to help?'

'Thank you, Remy, but I am good to go,' Grethe replied, gesturing to a large trolley. It was covered by a stiff white tablecloth and at its centre stood a most impressive Baumkuchen. It was nearly as tall as Chef Remy himself.

Grethe checked the clock on the wall. 'Henry said to wait fifteen minutes before we serve dessert, but I do not see the harm in wheeling it out to tantalise their tastebuds,' she said, her eyes sparkling.

Mr Walker was deep in the hunt for a fatty rind of bacon when he heard Grethe whistle for him to join her. He looked up and spotted the woman carefully backing out of the kitchen with the dessert trolley.

*Oops! Wait for me!* Mr Walker bounded towards her and, in his excitement, slipped on the tiles.

The kitchen doors swung to a close as Mr Walker scrabbled to regain his foot-hold. He galloped towards the exit at full speed. Little did he know that Grethe had halted on the other side of the doors to rearrange the tablecloth. Mr Walker barrelled through, straight into Grethe Schmidt . . . and her Baumkuchen.

## CHAPTER ELEVEN

The densely packed tree cake filled with intricate layers of ring upon ring of pastry seemed for a moment to grow wings of its own as it flew into the air.

Mr Walker skidded to a halt in the restaurant and watched on in horror.

Grethe whimpered as she stared, aghast, at the flying dessert she had spent over two days creating.

It was Remy who leapt into action. He indicated for the music to be turned up and beckoned Charlie over to them.

You see, it is moments like these that can make or break a hotel's staff. Over the years, Mr Walker would come to learn that it was the times when things do not go to plan that a staff member's reputation is forged. Charlie was to be known forever more as the tree-catcher.

For catch a tree cake he did!

Several layers had dislodged, so the cake looked more like a set of separate Olympic rings than a tree cake, but at least it hadn't ended up on the restaurant floor.

Mr Walker was devastated. *The dessert is ruined and it's all my fault*, he thought miserably.

With a professionalism beyond his station, Charlie managed to juggle the layers of cake back inside the safe confines of the kitchen, where they promptly fell apart into one giant heap of chocolate and pastry on the counter.

Thomas raced in through the swinging door. 'I'm guessing that wasn't the piece of entertainment the guests think it is?'

Remy shook his head. 'Not quite.'

'Not just that. We no longer have a dessert to serve,' Grethe said, unable to tear her gaze from the mess on the counter. 'If only I had thought to make a back-up. What am I to do?'

*A back-up?* Mr Walker had an idea. He padded over to Thomas and stuck his nose into the porter's jacket pocket. There was the familiar smell of ink and paper. Mr Walker pulled out the folded newspaper and pushed it into Thomas's hand.

'The crossword?' Thomas said. 'Now is not the time, Mr Walker. Perhaps we can look at it later.'

But Mr Walker was not to be deterred. He nudged the newspaper and gave a low whine.

Thomas eyed him curiously. He unfolded the newspaper and looked at the crossword. His eyebrows jumped up in surprise. 'Croquembouche?' he said. 'Do you want us to make a croquembouche?'

Mr Walker nodded and lifted his paw.

'That is a fine suggestion. It is my favourite dessert, after all,' Remy said, 'but we cannot make one now. It takes days to prepare as you need to make the profiteroles first.'

Grethe gasped and crouched down to hold Mr Walker's face with both hands. 'You are a genius! Thomas, I need you to fetch Mrs Reeves right away.'

Still uncertain as to what was going on, Thomas nodded and left the kitchen.

Grethe turned to Remy. 'Could you whip up spun sugar for a croquembouche?' she asked.

'Of course. I would be honoured to help,' Remy said, 'but what is it for if we are not making a croquembouche?'

'Trust me,' Grethe said with a wink. She met Mr Walker's gaze. 'I hope Henry can keep the crowd entertained while we see if we can pull this off.'

Henry needed no encouragement. In fact, he had a ball keeping the crowd of hotel guests entertained. Mr Walker gazed out at the sea of faces and could see so many friends. There were regular guests and old friends, such as Tracy Strizke, who was sitting at a table with colleagues and clients from Guide Dogs.

He noticed Grethe waving to him from the small window of the swinging door and bounded over to her.

Mr Walker could hardly believe his eyes when he entered. A very impressive tower of profiteroles was taking pride of place on the trolley. The choux pastry balls were held together with spun sugar and at their base was a sea of broken pieces of Baumkuchen. It looked and smelled very tasty.

Mrs Reeves, Sophie and Amanda looked flushed and breathless but, most of all,

pleased. They had been working hard to create the tower with Grethe. 'Ta-da!' they exclaimed proudly.

Remy beamed. 'We have made a brand-new dessert that is both French and German!'

Grethe clapped her hands together and laughed. 'The best of both worlds!'

Mr Walker looked up at the enormous dessert and felt his tummy rumble. Surely someone would allow him a taste?

Remy held open the door for Grethe. 'Now, let us try this again. After you, my dear,' he said with a sweeping bow.

'Why, thank you, Chef Remy.' Grethe giggled as she pushed the trolley through.

Mrs Reeves, the girls and Mr Walker followed. As they entered the restaurant, Mr Walker could hear the guests gasp at the sight of the towering dessert ... and then the delicious sound of applause.

# CHAPTER TWELVE

As the one hundred guests and staff tucked into their dessert with relish, all that could be heard were the happy sounds of spoons chinking against bowls and murmurs of delight. The Baum-Bouche, or the Croquem-Kuchen, was a resounding success and so was the hotel's anniversary party.

Grethe and Remy even shared a taste while sitting side by side on the kitchen bench with a pot of tea between them.

Mr Walker's spirits soared at the sight of Amanda carrying a small plate of dessert towards him. It looked utterly delicious. She placed the plate in front of Mr Walker and held her finger to her lips. He didn't need any encouragement. All too soon the dessert was off the plate and in his tummy, and he was doing a good job of licking the plate clean. Utterly delicious indeed.

# FRIENDS OF
## MR WALKER

| | |
|---|---|
| Mr Walker | *Labrador Ambassador* |
| Henry Reeves | *Hotel Manager* |
| Omid Abedini | *Head Concierge* |
| Monica Matthews | *Concierge* |
| Thomas Glover | *Porter* |
| Meraj Reddy | *Functions* |
| Remy Charron | *Head Chef* |
| Grethe Schmidt | *Pastry Chef* |
| Charlie | *Assistant Chef* |
| Elvis Duffy | *Housekeeping* |
| Rebecca Reeves | *Henry's wife, mother to Sophie and Amanda* |
| Sophie Reeves | *9-year-old daughter of Henry and Rebecca* |
| Amanda Reeves | *7-year-old daughter of Henry and Rebecca* |
| Tracy Strizke | *Guide Dogs Victoria* |

# ABOUT THE REAL MR WALKER

Born on 3 December 2015, Mr Walker was trained to provide assistance and companionship to people with low vision or blindness by Guide Dogs Victoria. After achieving many milestone stages in his training, it was decided that his larger-than-life personality was best suited to an ambassador role, where his affectionate nature would truly be able to shine.

Under the principal care of the hotel manager, who is also his official foster carer, Mr Walker has been calling Park Hyatt Melbourne home since 2017. Mr Walker quickly made a name for himself within the hotel as well as with the wider Melbourne community through daily meet-and-greets at the hotel lobby. He has rubbed shoulders with people from all walks of life, including celebrities, and even achieved his own celebrity status when *The Project* caught wind of the four-legged ambassador and aired him on their evening news.

Despite his rise to fame, Mr Walker prefers to spend most of his time within the hotel's serene grounds, nestled between parklands and elm-lined boulevards. His gentle nature shines most when he is greeting guests with a warm, furry welcome and making everyone at the hotel feel right at home.

# ABOUT GUIDE DOGS AUSTRALIA

Every hour of every day, an Australian family learns that their loved one will have severe or permanent sight-loss. Nine of these Australians will eventually go blind. It is estimated that there are over 450,000 Australians who are blind or have low vision and this number is expected to significantly increase with an ageing population.

Guide Dogs Australia, in collaboration with its state-based organisations, delivers essential services to children, teenagers and the elderly who are blind or have low vision in every state and territory across Australia. Their mission is to assist people who are blind or have low vision to gain the freedom and independence to move safely and confidently around their communities, and to fulfil their potential.

For more information about Guide Dogs Australia, visit guidedogsaustralia.com.au

**Jess Black** is an Australian author of children's books. She has written over thirty junior fiction books and two picture books, *Moon Dance* and *The Bold Australian Girl*. Jess is the author of the Keeper of the Crystals series and the Guide Dogs Australia Little Paws series, and is the co-author of the hugely successful Bindi Wildlife Adventure series and the RSPCA Animal Tales series.

**Sara Acton** is an award-winning author and illustrator of children's books. She lives on the Central Coast of New South Wales with one husband, two children, a mischievous dog and a cat called Poppy, who's definitely in charge.

*See how it all began in*

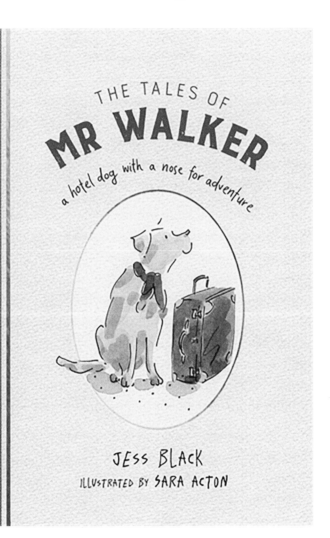

THE TALES OF

MR WALKER

a hotel dog with a nose for adventure

JESS BLACK

ILLUSTRATED BY SARA ACTON

*Available now*

# MR WALKER

## Gets the Inside Scoop

### JESS BLACK
Illustrated by Sara Acton

*Available now*

*You'll be able to join Mr Walker
on all sorts of new adventures in August 2019.
He can't wait!*